Books By
RATHER FUNNY PRESS

Would You Rather? For 6 Year Old Kids!
Would You Rather? For 7 Year Old Kids!
Would You Rather? For 8 Year Old Kids!
Would You Rather? For 9 Year Old Kids!
Would You Rather? For 10 Year Old Kids!
Would You Rather? For 11 Year Old Kids!
Would You Rather? For 12 Year Old Kids!
Would You Rather? For Teens!
Would You Rather? Eww! Yuck! Gross!

To see all the latest books by
Rather Funny Press just go to
RatherFunnyPress.com

YOUR FREE SURPRISE GIFT!

Details on the last page of this book!
A brand new free joke book
just for you.
Check it out! Laughter awaits!

RatherFunnyPress.com

HOW TO PLAY

This easy to play game is a ton of fun!
Have 2 or more players.
The first reader will choose a 'Would You Rather?'
from the book and read it aloud.
The other player(s) then choose which scenario
they would prefer and why.
You can't say 'neither' or 'none'.
You must choose one and explain why.
Then the book is passed to the next person
and the game continues!

The main rule is have fun, laugh and enjoy
spending time with your friends and family.
Let the fun begin!

ATTENTION!

All the scenarios and choices in this book are
fictional and meant to be about using your
imagination, having a ton of fun and enjoying this
game with your friends and family.
Obviously, DO NOT ATTEMPT any of these
scenarios in real life.

RatherFunnyPress.com

WOULD YOU RATHER...

HAVE GRAVITY TURN OFF FOR A DAY

OR

THE SUN TURN OFF FOR A WEEK?

HAVE EYES THAT ARE 4 TIMES AS BIG AS USUAL

OR

HAVE NORMAL SIZED EYES BUT YOU COULDN'T BLINK?

WOULD YOU RATHER...

BATTLE 20 TIGERS THE SIZE OF A RABBIT

OR

ONE RABBIT THE SIZE OF A TIGER?

HAVE EYES THAT CHANGE COLOR DEPENDING ON YOUR MOOD

OR

HAIR THAT CHANGES COLOR DEPENDING ON THE WEATHER?

WOULD YOU RATHER...

CUDDLE AN ANGRY
PARROT

OR

A RELAXED TIGER?

HAVE THE HEAD OF YOUR
TEACHER WITH YOUR BODY

OR

THE BODY OF YOUR TEACHER
WITH YOUR HEAD?

WOULD YOU RATHER...

HOLD A LIZARD

OR

KISS A SNAIL?

HAVE A FAST SPORTS CAR THAT CAN ONLY FIT 2 PEOPLE

OR

A SLOW LIMOUSINE THAT CAN FIT 8 PEOPLE?

WOULD YOU RATHER...

BE ATTACKED BY
DINOSAURS

OR

BY ALIENS?

WEAR THE SAME THING
EVERY DAY

OR

NEVER WEAR THE SAME
CLOTHES TWICE?

WOULD YOU RATHER...

WALK BAREFOOT FOR A MILE IN HOT SAND

OR

FREEZING COLD SNOW?

EVERYTHING IN YOUR HOUSE BE ONE COLOR

OR

EVERY SINGLE WALL AND DOOR BE A DIFFERENT COLOR?

WOULD YOU RATHER...

BE THE PILOT OF
A PLANE

OR

THE CAPTAIN OF A CRUISE
SHIP?

HAVE A BOWL OF ICE CREAM
FOR BREAKFAST

OR

A BOWL OF CANDY FOR
DINNER?

WOULD YOU RATHER...

HAVE A PARROT MAKE A
NEST IN YOUR HAIR

OR

5 SEAGULLS POOP IN
YOUR HAIR?

GO TO A FANCY
RESTAURANT

OR

AN ALL YOU CAN EAT
RESTAURANT?

WOULD YOU RATHER...

HAVE ONE HAND WITH 8 FINGERS

OR

ONE FOOT WITH 8 TOES?

HAVE A PORTAL TO A CHOCOLATE FACTORY

OR

THE MALL?

WOULD YOU RATHER...

HAVE A TINY HEAD COMPARED TO YOUR BODY

OR

HAVE A FURRY FACE?

BE STUCK IN AN AQUARIUM WITH A GREAT WHITE SHARK

OR

IN A ROOM WHERE THE FLOOR IS COVERED BY SPIDERS?

WOULD YOU RATHER...

MEET SOMEONE WHO HAS THREE EYES ON THEIR FOREHEAD

OR

TWO MOUTHS?

DISCOVER A REAL LIVING DINOSAUR IN YOUR BACKYARD

OR

A FRIENDLY ALIEN IN YOUR CLOSET?

WOULD YOU RATHER...

NEVER BE ABLE TO
EAT MEAT

OR

NEVER BE ABLE TO EAT
VEGETABLES?

HAVE TO USE A DIRTY
RESTROOM TOILET

OR

A SPARKLING CLEAN TOILET
THAT HAS A SNAKE IN IT?

WOULD YOU RATHER...

GO TO THE BEACH WHENEVER YOU WANT

OR

GO TO THE SNOW WHENEVER YOU WANT?

HAVE 3 TOES ON YOUR FACE INSTEAD OF A NOSE

OR

3 FINGERS ON EACH SIDE OF YOUR HEAD INSTEAD OF EARS?

WOULD YOU RATHER...

BE IN JAIL FOR A YEAR

OR

LOSE A YEAR OFF YOUR LIFE?

DANCE IN FRONT OF 1,000 PEOPLE

OR

SING IN FRONT OF 1,000 PEOPLE?

WOULD YOU RATHER...

BE A MERMAID THAT CAN WALK ON LAND

OR

AN OGRE THAT GETS THE PRINCESS?

INVITE YODA TO A DINNER PARTY AT YOUR HOUSE

OR

GEORGE WASHINGTON TO A DINNER PARTY AT YOUR HOUSE?

WOULD YOU RATHER...

BE ABLE TO SLOW DOWN TIME

OR

RUN INCREDIBLY FAST?

HAVE BRIGHT BLUE HAIR

OR

BRIGHT GREEN HAIR?

WOULD YOU RATHER...

SMILE WHEN YOU'RE SAD

OR

FROWN WHEN YOU'RE HAPPY?

CLEAN YOUR ROOM EVERY DAY AND NEVER DO HOMEWORK

OR

DO HOMEWORK EVERY DAY AND NEVER NEED TO CLEAN YOUR ROOM?

WOULD YOU RATHER...

RIDE IN A HOT AIR BALLOON

OR

IN A HOVERCRAFT?

GIVE UP BATHING FOR A MONTH

OR

GIVE UP THE INTERNET FOR A MONTH?

WOULD YOU RATHER...

BE IN PRISON FOR
20 YEARS

OR

HAVE NO ARMS?

FLY ANYWHERE YOU WANTED
FOR FREE

OR

EAT IN ANY RESTAURANT YOU
WANTED FOR FREE?

WOULD YOU RATHER...

EAT A SPOONFUL OF
FRIED INSECTS

OR

A SPOONFUL OF EXTREMELY
SPICY HOT SAUCE?

LIVE IN A MANSION IN
BEVERLY HILLS

OR

LIVE IN A PENTHOUSE IN
NEW YORK?

WOULD YOU RATHER...

BE POOR WITH LOTS OF
GOOD FRIENDS

OR

RICH WITH NO FRIENDS
AT ALL?

BE ABLE TO SHRINK DOWN
TO THE SIZE OF AN ANT
WHENEVER YOU WANT

OR

GROW TO THE SIZE OF A
TWO-STORY BUILDING
WHENEVER YOU WANT?

WOULD YOU RATHER...

HAVE A PET KANGAROO

OR

A PET SQUIRREL?

BE COVERED IN FUR

OR

COVERED IN FISH SCALES?

WOULD YOU RATHER...

HAVE A MAGICAL
FLYING CARPET

OR

A CAR THAT CAN DRIVE
UNDERWATER?

BE REALLY GOOD AT
MATH

OR

REALLY GOOD AT
SPORTS?

WOULD YOU RATHER...

LIVE AT AN AMUSEMENT PARK

OR

A BOWLING ALLEY?

LIVE IN A HOUSE MADE OF CHOCOLATE

OR

A HOUSE MADE OF PIZZA?

WOULD YOU RATHER...

GIVE UP YOUR CELL PHONE
FOR A MONTH

OR

YOUR FAVORITE PET
FOR A YEAR?

HAVE A NEVER-ENDING SUPPLY
OF ICE CREAM

OR

A NEVER-ENDING SUPPLY
OF KFC?

WOULD YOU RATHER...

LIVE IN A TREEHOUSE

OR

LIVE ON A BOAT?

NOT BE ABLE TO READ

OR

NOT BE ABLE TO SPEAK?

WOULD YOU RATHER...

RIDE IN A FERRARI

OR

ON A HORSE?

SWIM IN A POOL OF YOUR FAVORITE SODA

OR

SWIM IN A POOL OF MILK?

WOULD YOU RATHER...

LIVE IN THE HARRY POTTER WORLD

OR

THE STAR WARS WORLD?

BE ABLE TO FLY FOR ONE DAY

OR

BE SUPER STRONG FOR A WEEK?

WOULD YOU RATHER...

BE ABLE TO TYPE AND TEXT
VERY FAST

OR

READ REALLY QUICKLY?

BE GIVEN ONE MILLION DOLLARS
THAT YOU HAVE TO SPEND
IN A WEEK

OR

TEN THOUSAND DOLLARS
A MONTH FOR THE REST
OF YOUR LIFE?

WOULD YOU RATHER...

GET YOUR HAIR CUT BY A FIVE YEAR OLD GIRL

OR

BY AN 85 YEAR OLD WOMAN?

EAT 10 POUNDS OF CHOCOLATE

OR

DRINK 15 MILKSHAKES?

WOULD YOU RATHER...

DRINK A SMALL GLASS OF TABASCO SAUCE

OR

FILL YOUR MOUTH ENTIRELY WITH FRIED ANTS?

SPEAK EVERY LANGUAGE EXCEPT ENGLISH

OR

UNDERSTAND ENGLISH BUT YOU CAN ONLY RESPOND IN SIGN LANGUAGE?

WOULD YOU RATHER...

BE HARRY POTTER

OR

SUPERMAN?

EAT A BOWL OF SPAGHETTI NOODLES WITHOUT SAUCE

OR

A BOWL OF SPAGHETTI SAUCE WITHOUT NOODLES?

WOULD YOU RATHER...

TEACH HISTORY

OR

TEACH MATH?

LOSE YOUR BEST FRIEND

OR

ALL OF YOUR FRIENDS EXCEPT FOR YOUR BEST FRIEND?

WOULD YOU RATHER...

SWIM WITH A PIRANHA THE SIZE OF A WHALE

OR

50 WHALES THE SIZE OF A PIRANHA?

WRESTLE AN ALLIGATOR ONE TIME

OR

HAVE TO WEAR ONLY PINK FOR A YEAR?

WOULD YOU RATHER...

BE ABLE TO JUMP OVER
A TREE

OR

THROW A TREE?

GET A FREE APPETIZER WITH
EVERY MEAL

OR

A FREE DESSERT WITH
EVERY MEAL?

WOULD YOU RATHER...

HAVE A PET DINOSAUR

OR

A PET UNICORN?

HAVE EDIBLE SPAGHETTI HAIR THAT REGROWS EVERY NIGHT

OR

SWEAT CHOCOLATE MILK?

WOULD YOU RATHER...

WORK AS CABIN CREW ON INTERNATIONAL FLIGHTS

OR

WORK ON A CRUISE SHIP?

SLEEP FOR 5 HOURS EVERY NIGHT

OR

10 HOURS EVERY NIGHT?

WOULD YOU RATHER...

GO SWIMMING IN A RIVER OF MELTED CHOCOLATE

OR

DIVE INTO A POOL OF SODA?

HAVE HAIR THAT GROWS AT I FOOT A DAY

OR

BE COMPLETELY BALD?

WOULD YOU RATHER...

BE ABLE TO CONTROL ANIMALS (BUT NOT HUMANS) WITH YOUR MIND

OR

CONTROL ELECTRONICS WITH YOUR MIND?

LISTEN TO RAP MUSIC

OR

COUNTRY MUSIC?

WOULD YOU RATHER...

WEAR CLOWN SHOES EVERY DAY

OR

A CLOWN WIG EVERY DAY?

FIGHT THREE BULLS AT THE SAME TIME

OR

FIGHT TEN BULLS ONE AT A TIME?

WOULD YOU RATHER...

EAT THE HOTTEST PEPPER
IN THE WORLD

OR

EAT ICE CREAM MADE
FROM DIRT?

NOT BE ABLE TO SHOWER OR
BATH FOR A YEAR

OR

NOT BE ABLE TO WASH YOUR
CLOTHES FOR A YEAR?

WOULD YOU RATHER...

GET STUNG BY A BEE

OR

SCRATCHED BY A CAT?

BE ABLE TO MOVE SILENTLY
LIKE A NINJA

OR

HAVE AN INCREDIBLY LOUD
AND SCARY VOICE?

WOULD YOU RATHER...

HAVE ONE REALLY
BIG EYE

OR

ONE REALLY BIG EAR?

HOLD A POISONOUS SNAKE
FOR AN HOUR

OR

A HUGE TARANTULA FOR
AN HOUR?

WOULD YOU RATHER...

GO TO THE MOON

OR

CLIMB MT EVEREST?

HAVE EYES THAT WORKED LIKE BINOCULARS TO SEE FAR AWAY

OR

EYES THAT WORKED LIKE A MICROSCOPE TO SEE REALLY CLOSE UP?

WOULD YOU RATHER...

HAVE NO HAIR AT ALL

OR

HAVE BRIGHT RED HAIR WITH BLUE POLKA DOTS?

GO ON A COOL HOLIDAY WITH YOUR FAMILY

OR

HAVE $100 TO SPEND AT THE MALL?

WOULD YOU RATHER...

DIG UP A PIRATE TREASURE CHEST IN YOUR BACKYARD

OR

DIG UP A DINOSAUR SKELETON?

SLEEP ON THE SOFA FOR A YEAR

OR

BUY A NEW BED EVERY WEEK?

WOULD YOU RATHER...

HAVE 2 HANDS AT THE END OF EACH ARM

OR

2 FEET AT THE END OF EACH LEG?

MAKE THE WORLD'S BIGGEST PIZZA

OR

THE WORLD'S BIGGEST PANCAKE?

WOULD YOU RATHER...

BE ON AN EMPTY BEACH
IN WINTER

OR

A REALLY BUSY BEACH
IN SUMMER?

HAVE OUT OF CONTROL
BODY HAIR

OR

A STRONG, PUNGENT
BODY ODOR?

WOULD YOU RATHER...

WALK ACROSS A MILE OF HOT COALS

OR

A MILE OF LEGOS?

NEVER BRUSH YOUR TEETH AGAIN

OR

NEVER WASH YOUR HAIR AGAIN?

WOULD YOU RATHER...

HAVE ONE REALLY LONG LEG

OR

ONE REALLY LONG ARM?

HAVE A PET CAT THAT CAN SPEAK ENGLISH

OR

A PET DOG THAT IS BIG ENOUGH TO RIDE?

WOULD YOU RATHER...

NOT BE ABLE TO SIT

OR

NOT BE ABLE TO STAND?

HAVE AN ALIEN SHARE YOUR ROOM FOR A MONTH

OR

GO TO THE ALIEN'S PLANET FOR A MONTH?

WOULD YOU RATHER...

MAKE A HOUSE OUT OF CHEESEBURGERS

OR

A FORT OUT OF CUPCAKES?

HAVE A MULTICOLORED HEAD

OR

A TWO FOOT LONG TAIL?

WOULD YOU RATHER...

HAVE A FLYING CAR

OR

A SEE-THROUGH SUBMARINE?

MEET A CAT THAT WALKS ON TWO LEGS

OR

A CAT THAT TALKS?

WOULD YOU RATHER...

SPEND A WEEK IN SPACE

OR

SPEND A WEEK ON THE BOTTOM OF THE OCEAN?

NEVER BE ABLE TO DRINK SODA AGAIN

OR

ONLY BE ABLE TO DRINK SODA AND NOTHING ELSE?

WOULD YOU RATHER...

BE AN INCREDIBLY FAST SWIMMER

OR

AN INCREDIBLY HIGH JUMPER?

SING AT THE TOP OF YOUR VOICE FOR 10 SECONDS

OR

DO A CRAZY DANCE FOR 30 SECONDS EVERY TIME YOU MEET SOMEONE NEW?

WOULD YOU RATHER...

HAVE TO READ ALOUD EVERY WORD YOU READ

OR

SING EVERYTHING YOU SAY OUT LOUD?

HAVE A TAIL THAT WAGS WHEN YOU ARE HAPPY

OR

A NOSE THAT GROWS WHEN YOU TELL A LIE?

WOULD YOU RATHER...

TRAIN A WHALE SIZED
GOLDFISH

OR

A GOLDFISH SIZED WHALE?

HAVE THE HEAD OF
A FLY

OR

THE LEGS OF A CHICKEN?

WOULD YOU RATHER...

BE A FAMOUS WRITER

OR

A FAMOUS INVENTOR?

WAKE UP WITH EAGLE WINGS

OR

PENGUIN FLIPPERS?

WOULD YOU RATHER...

HAVE MILK LEAK FROM YOUR NOSE EVERY TIME YOU LAUGHED

OR

CRY MILK FROM YOUR EYES EVERY TIME YOU SNEEZED?

TAKE A SIZZLING HOT SHOWER

OR

A FREEZING COLD SHOWER?

WOULD YOU RATHER...

HAVE 20 MILLION YOUTUBE SUBSCRIBERS

OR

MAKE A BLOCKBUSTER ACTION MOVIE?

RANDOMLY TURN INTO A FROG FOR A DAY ONCE A MONTH

OR

RANDOMLY TURN INTO A BIRD FOR A DAY ONCE EVERY WEEK?

WOULD YOU RATHER...

WIN AN OLYMPIC GOLD MEDAL

OR

AN ACADEMY AWARD?

PLAY NINTENDO FOR 3 HOURS

OR

PLAYSTATION FOR 2 HOURS?

WOULD YOU RATHER...

CLIMB A MOUNTAIN

OR

DO A 10 FEET DIVE INTO A POOL?

BE A TEACHER

OR

A DOCTOR?

WOULD YOU RATHER...

TRY TO FLY A KITE IN
A HURRICANE

OR

A SNOWSTORM?

HAVE NINJA SKILLS

OR

HAVE AMAZING CODING
SKILLS IN ANY COMPUTER
LANGUAGE?

WOULD YOU RATHER...

VACATION IN AUSTRALIA

OR

VACATION IN HAWAII?

EAT A SPOONFUL OF SUGAR

OR

A SPOONFUL OF SALT?

WOULD YOU RATHER...

START A COLONY ON ANOTHER PLANET

OR

BE THE LEADER OF A SMALL COUNTRY ON EARTH?

WORK IN A REALLY BORING JOB THAT PAID WELL

OR

A REALLY EXCITING JOB THAT DIDN'T PAY AS MUCH?

WOULD YOU RATHER...

EAT 50 CHICKEN NUGGETS

OR

4 BIG MACS?

GET CHASED BY ONE ANGRY SHEEP

OR

12 ANGRY SQUIRRELS?

WOULD YOU RATHER...

BE ABLE TO CONTROL THE WIND AT WILL

OR

BE ABLE TO CONTROL FIRE?

BE STUCK IN A HURRICANE

OR

EXPERIENCE AN EARTHQUAKE?

WOULD YOU RATHER...

HAVE REALLY COLD
WEATHER

OR

REALLY HOT WEATHER?

ONLY BE ABLE TO WALK
ON ALL FOURS

OR

ONLY BE ABLE TO WALK
SIDEWAYS LIKE A CRAB?

WOULD YOU RATHER...

CHANGE THE COLOR OF YOUR HAIR

OR

YOUR EYES?

RIDE A DONKEY TO SCHOOL

OR

A GIRAFFE TO SCHOOL?

WOULD YOU RATHER...

BE YODA

OR

DARTH VADER?

BE ABLE TO CREATE A
NEW HOLIDAY

OR

CREATE A NEW SPORT?

WOULD YOU RATHER...

GO TO THE OLYMPICS TO DO GYMNASTICS

OR

PLAY BASKETBALL?

LIVE ON A SAILING BOAT

OR

IN A SMALL CABIN IN THE MOUNTAINS?

WOULD YOU RATHER...

GIVE UP WATCHING TV AND MOVIES FOR A YEAR

OR

GIVE UP VIDEO GAMES FOR A YEAR?

HAVE CHEWING GUM STUCK IN YOUR HAIR

OR

CHEWING GUM STUCK UP YOUR NOSE?

WOULD YOU RATHER...

HAVE A FOOD FIGHT AGAINST YOUR BEST FRIEND

OR

YOUR DAD?

EAT ONLY WITH A SPOON FOR THE REST OF YOUR LIFE

OR

ONLY WITH A FORK FOR THE REST OF YOUR LIFE?

WOULD YOU RATHER...

LIVE IN THE WILDERNESS FOR THE REST OF YOUR LIFE

OR

HAVE NO LEGS?

GET A HAIRCUT EVERY SINGLE DAY FOR 5 YEARS

OR

NEVER HAVE A HAIRCUT FOR 5 YEARS?

WOULD YOU RATHER...

DISCOVER A NEW ELEMENT AND NAME IT AFTER YOURSELF

OR

WIN GOLD AT THE OLYMPIC GAMES?

HAVE UNLIMITED INTERNATIONAL FIRST-CLASS TICKETS

OR

NEVER HAVE TO PAY FOR FOOD AT RESTAURANTS AGAIN?

WOULD YOU RATHER...

TRAVEL THE WORLD FOR A YEAR ALL EXPENSES PAID

OR

HAVE $20,000 TO SPEND ON WHATEVER YOU WANT?

BE ABLE TO SEE 10 MINUTES INTO YOUR OWN FUTURE

OR

10 MINUTES INTO THE FUTURE OF ANYONE BUT YOURSELF?

WOULD YOU RATHER...

BE ABLE TO CREATE PORTALS

OR

CONTROL GRAVITY?

LIVE IN AN ACTION MOVIE

OR

IN A DISNEY CARTOON?

WOULD YOU RATHER...

BE ALLERGIC TO
DOGS

OR

ALLERGIC TO CATS?

NOT BE ABLE TO STOP
DANCING

OR

NOT BE ABLE TO STOP
SINGING?

WOULD YOU RATHER...

WIN ONE THOUSAND DOLLARS

OR

NEVER HAVE TO DO HOMEWORK EVER AGAIN?

BE ABLE TO TELEPORT ANYWHERE

OR

BE ABLE TO READ MINDS?

WOULD YOU RATHER...

HAVE A COMPLETELY
AUTOMATED HOME

OR

A SELF-DRIVING CAR?

BE A CHARACTER IN YOUR
FAVOURITE GAME

OR

A CHARACTER IN YOUR
FAVOURITE MOVIE?

WOULD YOU RATHER...

HAVE AN AIR HOCKEY TABLE

OR

A PINBALL MACHINE?

BE BAREFOOT FOR THE REST OF YOUR LIFE

OR

WEAR HIGH HEELS FOR THE REST OF YOUR LIFE?

WOULD YOU RATHER...

TRAVEL ALL OVER THE WORLD

OR

VISIT THE MOON AND MARS?

VISIT THE INTERNATIONAL SPACE STATION FOR A WEEK

OR

STAY IN AN UNDERWATER HOTEL FOR A WEEK?

WOULD YOU RATHER...

SKYDIVE

OR

BUNGEE JUMP?

HOLD A SNAKE FOR
2 HOURS

OR

4 REALLY BIG SPIDERS
FOR 1 HOUR?

WOULD YOU RATHER...

HAVE AN EMBARRASSING FALL IN PUBLIC

OR

FART LOUDLY IN PUBLIC?

BE A JEDI WITHOUT A LIGHTSABER

OR

BE A WIZARD WITHOUT A WAND?

WOULD YOU RATHER...

HAVE A HORSE'S TAIL

OR

A UNICORN HORN?

HAVE NO INTERNET FOR
A MONTH

OR

NO CELL PHONE FOR
A WEEK?

WOULD YOU RATHER...

NEVER LISTEN TO MUSIC AGAIN

OR

NEVER WATCH TV AGAIN?

SIT IN A ROOM FULL OF COCKROACHES

OR

A ROOM FULL OF FLYING BIRDS?

WOULD YOU RATHER...

BE ALLERGIC TO PIZZA

OR

ALLERGIC TO CHOCOLATE?

STAND ON A FROZEN LAKE
WITH LOTS OF CRACKS

OR

WALK ON A TIGHTROPE AT
THE CIRCUS?

WOULD YOU RATHER...

EVERY SINGLE THING YOU ATE FROM NOW ON TASTED LIKE JELLY BEANS

OR

CHOCOLATE?

BE UNABLE TO TALK

OR

ONLY BE ABLE TO TALK LIKE SHAKESPEARE?

WOULD YOU RATHER...

HAVE THE CHANCE TO DESIGN A NEW TOY

OR

CREATE A NEW TV SHOW?

HAVE 15 EYEBROWS SPREAD ALL OVER YOUR FACE

OR

2 BRIGHT BLUE EYEBROWS?

WOULD YOU RATHER...

HAVE BOTH LEGS STUCK IN THE TOILET BOWL

OR

HAVE BOTH HANDS STUCK IN THE TOILET BOWL?

WEAR YOUR GRANDMA'S CLOTHES

OR

DRESS LIKE A BABY IN DIAPERS ON THE FIRST DAY AT A NEW SCHOOL?

WOULD YOU RATHER...

HAVE A NEW SILLY HAT APPEAR IN YOUR CLOSET EVERY MORNING

OR

A NEW PAIR OF SHOES APPEAR IN YOUR CLOSET ONCE A WEEK?

EAT SNAIL FLAVORED ICE CREAM

OR

DRINK ROTTEN WORM FLAVORED SODA?

WOULD YOU RATHER?

EWW! YUCK! GROSS!

This way to crazy, ridiculous and downright hilarious 'Would You Rathers?!'

WARNING!

These are Eww! These are Yuck! These are Gross! And they are really funny! Laughter awaits!

RatherFunnyPress.com

WOULD YOU RATHER...

FART IN FRONT OF YOUR TEACHER

OR

FART LOUDLY IN A LIBRARY?

PICK LINT OUT OF YOUR GRANDMA'S BELLY BUTTON

OR

PICK EAR WAX OUT OF YOUR GRANDPA'S EARS?

WOULD YOU RATHER...

FALL DOWN A STAIRCASE
MADE OF DEAD RATS

OR

MICROWAVE A DEAD RAT
AND USE IT AS A
HOT WATER BOTTLE?

SWIM TEN MILES THROUGH
THE SEWER

OR

HAVE EVERY SONG YOU EVER
HEAR FROM NOW ON BE MADE
ENTIRELY OF FART SOUNDS?

WOULD YOU RATHER...

HAVE ANTS CRAWLING ALL THROUGH YOUR ARMPITS

OR

SUCK ON A STRANGER'S USED HANDKERCHIEF?

PUT A LIVE CRAB DOWN YOUR UNDERPANTS

OR

DRINK A FULL CUP OF ROTTEN CRAB JUICE THROUGH YOUR NOSE?

WOULD YOU RATHER...

SWIM IN A POOL OF ROTTING FISH

OR

SIT IN A BATH OF SOUR MILK?

LICK YOUR OWN TOILET SEAT

OR

EAT A MEAL OFF A PUBLIC RESTROOM TOILET SEAT?

WOULD YOU RATHER...

DO A FART SO BIG IT CREATES
A MUSHROOM CLOUD

OR

NEVER DO ANOTHER FART
AGAIN BUT YOU POOP
TWICE AS MUCH?

PLAY IN A MUD PIT FILLED
WITH WORMS AND
3 MYSTERIOUS POOPS

OR

PLAY IN A BATH OF BAKED
BEANS AND BOOGERS?

WOULD YOU RATHER...

KISS A FROG ON THE LIPS

OR

SWIM IN A SMELLY, DIRTY POND THAT SMELLS LIKE FARTS?

ONLY BE ABLE TO DRINK THE PUS FROM POPPED PIMPLES FOR A WEEK

OR

HAVE A BATH IN 10% ELEPHANT PEE?

WOULD YOU RATHER...

CHALLENGE A FLATULENT OCTOPUS TO A FARTING COMPETITION

OR

EAT A GROSS SMELLING HOTDOG FROM A BIN?

HAVE 17 FRIED COCKROACHES FOR BREAKFAST EVERY MORNING

OR

HAVE TO SLEEP WITH 17 COCKROACHES CRAWLING ALL OVER YOU EVERY NIGHT?

WOULD YOU RATHER...

HAVE A HAPPY, ELDERLY LADY SNEEZE IN YOUR FACE

OR

FART ON YOUR FACE?

SKYDIVE INTO A PILE OF DIRTY DIAPERS AND NOT BE INJURED

OR

BOUNCE ON A TRAMPOLINE AND BREAK YOUR ARM?

WOULD YOU RATHER...

EAT A SNAIL ALIVE

OR

DO A FART IN A HAT AND THEN WEAR IT?

HAVE A BIG GRIZZLY BEAR DO A FART IN YOUR BED

OR

HAVE TO GO ONE YEAR WITHOUT WATCHING TV?

WOULD YOU RATHER...

PICK YOUR TEACHER'S NOSE

OR

CLIP THEIR TOENAILS?

STEP ON A POO WHILE
RUNNING BAREFOOT
AT THE BEACH

OR

HAVE A POO FLOAT BY WHILE
RELAXING IN A HOT TUB?

THANKS A BUNCH!

For reading our book!
We hope you have enjoyed these
'WOULD YOU RATHER?'
scenarios as much as we did as we were
putting this book together.
If you could possibly leave a review of our
book we would really appreciate it. ☺

To see all our latest books or leave a review
just go to
RatherFunnyPress.com
Once again, thanks so much for reading!

P.S. If you enjoyed the bonus chapter,
EWW! YUCK! GROSS!
you can always check out our brand new book,

WOULD YOU RATHER?
EWW! YUCK! GROSS!
for hundreds of brand new, crazy and ridiculous
scenarios that are sure to get the kids rolling on the
floor with laughter!
Just go to:
RatherFunnyPress.com
Thanks again! ☺

YOUR FREE SURPRISE GIFT!

HILARIOUS JOKES FOR CLEVER KIDS!

RATHER FUNNY PRESS

To grab your free copy of this brand new, hilarious Joke Book, just go to:

go.RatherFunnyPress.com

Enjoy!

RatherFunnyPress.com

Made in the USA
Middletown, DE
03 December 2022

16840186R00064